H·E·B read 3

GROW YOUNG MINDS, READ 3 TIMES A WEEK

H-E-B is strongly committed to improving education in Texas and has supported Texas schools through the Excellence in Education Awards program for more than 10 years. In 2011, when H-E-B learned that Texas was facing a major challenge regarding early childhood education and kindergarten readiness, H-E-B started the Read 3 Early Childhood Literacy Campaign.

Read 3's goals are to provide easy and affordable access to books for Texas families and encourage families to read to their early learners at least three times every week. Reading to a child improves his literacy, and when a child's literacy improves, she is more likely to succeed in school, less likely to drop out, and more likely to finish college. That's a brighter future for the child, the family, and for Texas.

Commit to reading at least three times a week to your early learner. Take the Read 3 Pledge!

"A, B, C and 1, 2, 3 – Reading is fun for me.
It helps me grow my young mind.
This week I pledge to read 3 times!"

Disney

This book belongs to

_____

Adapted from the original story by Lyn Calder
Illustrated by Adam DeVaney

Published by Bendon, Inc.

Printed in China

Disney MINNIE

Where's Fifi?

One lovely day, Minnie Mouse was walking her dog Fifi, when she saw a sign posted on a fence. "Oh, look, Fifi," she said. "A dog show—with prizes! You should enter!"

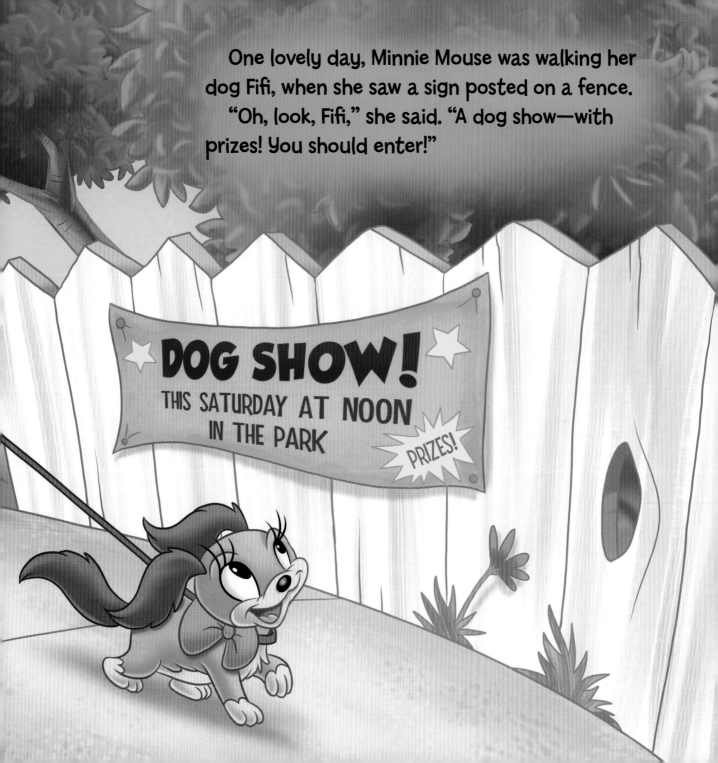

DOG SHOW!
THIS SATURDAY AT NOON
IN THE PARK
PRIZES!

Minnie and Fifi went straight
home to practice for the show.
"Fifi, sit!" said Minnie.
Fifi sat.
"Shake."
Fifi held up a paw.

"Good girl!" said Minnie, shaking
the dainty paw. "Now, roll over."
Fifi sat up. "Arf!"

"No, no," said Minnie. "You're supposed to bark when I say *Speak*."

Fifi rolled over.

"Oh, my," said Minnie. "We've got work to do. And the show is only two days away."

On the morning of the dog show, Minnie gave Fifi
a bath and dressed her in a red polka-dot bow.
"Now we match!" said Minnie happily. She proudly
walked Fifi down the lane toward the town square.

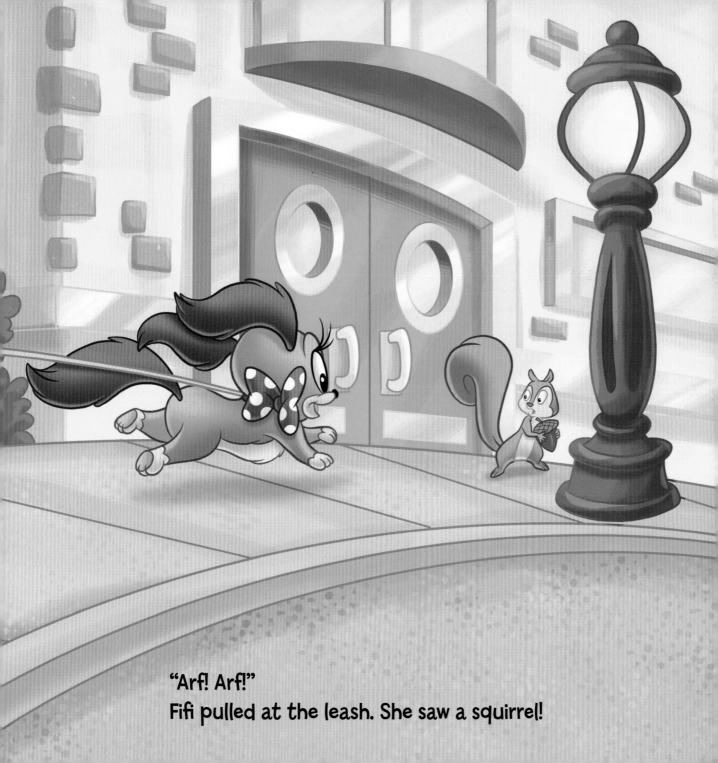

"Arf! Arf!"
Fifi pulled at the leash. She saw a squirrel!

Fifi squirmed and tugged, but Minnie held on tight.
Suddenly, Fifi slipped right out of her collar. Minnie
watched in surprise as the squirrel disappeared
around a corner—followed by a red polka-dot bow!
    "Fifi!" cried Minnie. "Come back!"

Minnie raced after Fifi. She turned the corner, but Fifi was nowhere in sight.

Minnie searched and searched for her sweet little dog. "Oh, Fifi," she said, "where can you be?"

She called her friend Daisy
and told her Fifi was lost.

"I'll be right there!"
announced Daisy.
"And I'll bring Mickey!"

When Daisy and Mickey arrived, they found Minnie crying. "And Fifi looked so pretty in her new bow, too," she said. "Don't worry, Minnie," said Mickey. "We'll help you find her." "That's right," Daisy agreed. "Let's get busy!"

Daisy called the town animal shelter right away.

"I want to report a missing dog," she said. "Her name is Fifi. When she disappeared, she was very clean—and she was wearing a red polka-dot bow."

Daisy gave Minnie's phone number to the people at the shelter, in case they found Fifi.

Minnie and Mickey made
lots of signs that read:

Minnie and her friends went all around the neighborhood,
calling for Fifi and posting the signs.

"Now let's go back to your house, Minnie,"
suggested Daisy. "Fifi may have found her way home."
"Thank you both for helping me," said Minnie.
"We love Fifi, too," said Mickey.

But when they reached Minnie's house,
there was no little dog.
"Poor Fifi," Minnie said. "She's lost
somewhere. I just don't know what to do."

"Well, I know what to do!" proclaimed Daisy. "I'm sending a message to all my friends: **We have lost a sweet little tan and cream dog with a red polka-dot bow. If you see her, please send a message back to me!**"

"Great thinking!" cheered Mickey.

"Oh, thank you," said Minnie. "You two are such good friends."

Within minutes, Daisy started getting messages back.

I'll go out and look!

Poor thing. I'll keep an eye out.

Sure thing, Daisy!

Hey, Daisy! Does she look like this?

A picture came up on Daisy's phone.
It was of a dog.
A cute dog with a red polka-dot bow!
And a big blue ribbon!

"It's Fifi! It's Fifi!" Minnie cried.

Daisy sent a message back: **Yes! That's Fifi! Where is she?**

The answer came. "She's at the dog show!" Daisy said.

Minnie raced away to the park with Daisy and Mickey right behind.

"Arf! Arf!"
Fifi barked when she saw Minnie coming.
"Oh, Fifi, I was so worried about you!"
said Minnie. "How did you get here?
And how did you win a blue ribbon?"

One of the judges explained. "Your dog arrived just as we began the judging," he said. "Every time someone said *Sit*, your dog sat. Every time someone said *Shake*, your dog held up her paw. She was so well behaved, we just *had* to give her the prize."

Minnie smiled. "You silly little dog," she said.
"You're lucky none of the judges said *Roll over*."
Fifi sat up. "Arf!"
Minnie giggled and hugged her prize-winning dog.